rge

shrinks

by WILLIAM JOYCE

LAURA GERINGER BOOKS

An Imprint of HarperCollins Publishers

One day, while his mother and father were out, George dreamt he was small, and when he woke up he found it was true.

His parents had left him a note. It read:

"Dear George, when you wake up,

please make your bed,

brush your teeth,

and take a bath.

Then clean up your room

and go get your little brother.

Eat a good breakfast,

and don't forget to wash the dishes, dear.

Do your homework.

Take out the garbage,

and play quietly.

Make sure you water the plants

and feed the fish.

Then check the mail

and get some fresh air.

Try to stay out of trouble,

and we'll be home soon.

Love, Mom and Dad."

for
Nate

New edition 2000
Copyright © 1985 by William Joyce
All rights reserved.
Manufactured in China.
Library of Congress Cataloging-in-Publication Data
Joyce, William.
George shrinks.
Summary: Taking care of a cat and a baby brother turns into a series of comic
adventures when George wakes up to find himself shrunk to the size of a mouse.
1. Children's stories, American. [1. Size—Fiction.] I. Title
PZ7.J857Ge 1985   [E]   83-47697
ISBN 0-06-023070-3 — ISBN 0-06-443129-0 (pbk.)
Typography by Alicia Mikles